TIME WARP TRIP™

vol. **2**

THE SEVEN BLUNDERS OF THE WORLD

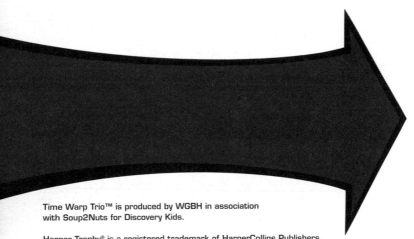

Time Warp Trio™ is produced by WGBH in association
with Soup2Nuts for Discovery Kids.

Harper Trophy® is a registered trademark of HarperCollins Publishers.

Time Warp Trio®
Time Warp Trio: The Seven Blunders of the World
Copyright © 2006 WGBH Educational Foundation and Chucklebait, Inc.
Artwork, Designs and Animation © 2005 WGBH Educational Foundation

For information address HarperCollins Children's Books,
a division of HarperCollins Publishers,
1350 Avenue of the Americas, New York, NY 10019.
www.harpercollinschildrens.com

Library of Congress catalog card number: 2006924549
ISBN-10: 0-06-111637-8 — ISBN-13: 978-0-06-111637-7

Book design by Joe Merkel
❖
First Harper Trophy edition, 2006

TIME WARP TRIP™

vol. **2**

THE SEVEN BLUNDERS OF THE WORLD

CREATED BY
JON SCIESZKA

ADAPTED BY
ZACHARY RAU

ADAPTED FROM THE
TELEPLAY BY
GARY APPLE

HarperTrophy®
An Imprint of HarperCollins*Publishers*

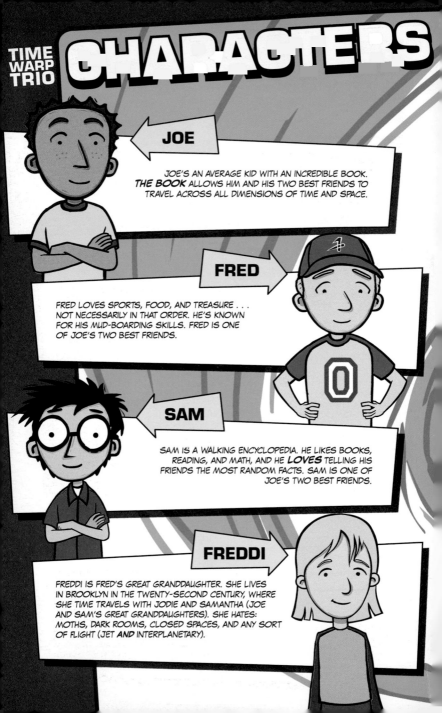

TIME WARP TRIO CHARACTERS

JOE

JOE'S AN AVERAGE KID WITH AN INCREDIBLE BOOK. *THE BOOK* ALLOWS HIM AND HIS TWO BEST FRIENDS TO TRAVEL ACROSS ALL DIMENSIONS OF TIME AND SPACE.

FRED

FRED LOVES SPORTS, FOOD, AND TREASURE . . . NOT NECESSARILY IN THAT ORDER. HE'S KNOWN FOR HIS MUD-BOARDING SKILLS. FRED IS ONE OF JOE'S TWO BEST FRIENDS.

SAM

SAM IS A WALKING ENCYCLOPEDIA. HE LIKES BOOKS, READING, AND MATH, AND HE *LOVES* TELLING HIS FRIENDS THE MOST RANDOM FACTS. SAM IS ONE OF JOE'S TWO BEST FRIENDS.

FREDDI

FREDDI IS FRED'S GREAT GRANDDAUGHTER. SHE LIVES IN BROOKLYN IN THE TWENTY-SECOND CENTURY, WHERE SHE TIME TRAVELS WITH JODIE AND SAMANTHA (JOE AND SAM'S GREAT GRANDDAUGHTERS). SHE HATES: MOTHS, DARK ROOMS, CLOSED SPACES, AND ANY SORT OF FLIGHT (JET *AND* INTERPLANETARY).

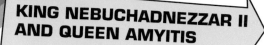

KING NEBUCHADNEZZAR II AND QUEEN AMYITIS

LIVED BETWEEN 625 B.C.E. AND B.C.E. 562 IN MESOPOTAMIA. THE KING WAS ALSO KNOWN AS "NEBUCHADNEZZAR THE GREAT". IN THE BIBLE, HE LOST "THE GREAT" AFTER HE DESTROYED THE TEMPLES OF JERUSALEM AND CONQUERED OTHER AREAS. HE BUILT THE HANGING GARDENS OF BABYLON FOR HIS WIFE, QUEEN AMYITIS, TO REMIND HER OF THE MOUNTAINS OF HER HOMELAND.

HAMMONRI

HAMMONRI IS UP TO NO GOOD! HE FOLLOWS ORDERS FROM A SIX-FOOT-TALL STONE STATUE OF MARDUK, THE BABYLONIAN SUN GOD. MARDUK TELLS HIM TO TRAVEL THROUGH TIME AND STEAL **THE BOOK** FROM JOE. HE CAN BE SEEN HANGING AROUND THE ZIGGURAT, OR TEMPLE TOWER.

MAD JACK

WATCH OUT FOR MAD JACK! WHETHER HE'S LURKING IN THE SHADOWS OR WANDERING ABOUT FREELY BEING MAD, HE'S UP TO NO GOOD. WHY'S HE SO MAD? IT MAY HAVE SOMETHING TO DO WITH HIS GOAL OF BECOMING "THE RULER OF ALL SPACE AND TIME."

THE BOOK

JOE RECEIVED **THE BOOK** AS A BIRTHDAY PRESENT FROM HIS UNCLE JOE. IT CAN WARP ANYONE TO ANY TIME AND ANY PLACE IN HISTORY. WHILE THAT SOUNDS REALLY COOL, THERE'S ONE PROBLEM: THE ONLY WAY TO GET BACK TO WHERE YOU CAME FROM IS TO FIND **THE BOOK** IN THE TIME AND PLACE YOU WARPED INTO. AND WHENEVER **THE BOOK** IS USED FOR TIME TRAVEL, IT HAS A HABIT OF DISAPPEARING.

THE BOYS LEAVE THE ROOM, UNAWARE OF THE ODD GLOWING BALL OVER JOE'S BED.

Zzzzzzzsssssshhh!!

THE BALL SUDDENLY POPS . . .

POP!

. . . AND A STRANGE MAN FALLS TO THE FLOOR.

SLAM!!

Ooof!

GREAT GILGAMESH!

IT'S JUST HOW MARDUK DESCRIBED IT!

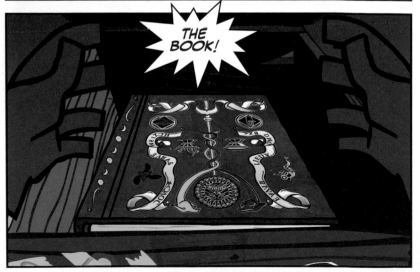

HAMMONRI ACTIVATES *THE BOOK* AND A GREEN MIST BEGINS TO SWIRL AROUND HIM.

HOUDINI

OT NOLYBAB!*

*EDITOR'S NOTE: "OT NOLYBAB" IS "TO BABYLON" BACKWARD.

HE'S PULLED INTO THE GREEN MIST . . .

. . . AND IS GONE!

SPLOOOOoosh!

OUTSIDE THE TEMPLE, HAMMONRI HAS COME TO SEE MARDUK, THE BABYLONIAN SUN GOD.

I HAVE BROUGHT WHAT YOU REQUESTED, GREAT MARDUK!

EXCELLENT!

WELL . . .

WHY ARE YOU JUST STANDING THERE, SWEATING ALL OVER MY TEMPLE FLOOR?!

BRING IT TO ME!

HAMMONRI PANICS AS HE REALIZES THAT HE DOESN'T HAVE *THE BOOK*.

UMMM . . . ?

IN PRESENT-DAY BROOKLYN, THE BOYS ARE TRYING TO FIGURE OUT WHO STOLE *THE BOOK.*

AND YOU'RE SURE ANNA DOESN'T HAVE IT?

POSITIVE! SHE WOULD HAVE TALKED IF SHE KNEW SOMETHING.

IT LOOKS LIKE THE LATCH WAS TORN OFF WITH A KNIFE. MAYBE THERE'S SOME EVIDENCE AROUND HERE.

EXCUSE ME, SHERLOCK, BUT I'M SURE WHOEVER STOLE *THE BOOK* WOULD BE SMART ENOUGH NOT TO LEAVE A TOOLBOX BEHIND.

HEY, WHAT'S THIS?

IT'S LIKE SOME KIND OF CODE.

IT'S CUNEIFORM— ONE OF THE OLDEST WRITTEN LANGUAGES IN THE WORLD. WE LEARNED ABOUT THIS IN HISTORY CLASS.

CAN YOU READ IT?

NO, BUT I KNOW CUNEIFORM WAS USED IN MESOPOTAMIA MORE THAN TWO THOUSAND YEARS AGO.

THAT'S TWO-THOUSAND-YEAR-OLD WRITING?? WHO WOULD BE WALKING AROUND WITH THAT IN HIS POCKET?

AN ARCHAEOLOGIST?

OR ANOTHER TIME-WARPER.

19

OUR LAW SAYS, "AN EYE FOR AN EYE, AND A TOOTH FOR A TOOTH." YOU TOOK SOMETHING FROM ME. NOW I WILL TAKE SOMETHING FROM YOU!

YOUR LIVES!

AAAAAAAAH!

THE KING AND QUEEN!!

27

WAIT! REMEMBER WHAT WE TALKED ABOUT?!

IF YOU WANT TO BE A POPULAR KING, YOU CAN'T JUST GO AROUND EXECUTING PEOPLE! AT LEAST FIND OUT WHAT THEY'VE SUPPOSEDLY STOLEN!

OH, ALL RIGHT!

IT'S JUST A GIFT FROM MY UNCLE. IT'S NOTHING SPECIAL REALLY.

CUNEIFORM, ONE OF THE WORLD'S **OLDEST** WRITING SYSTEMS, USED SHARPENED REEDS TO DRAW IN MOIST CLAY TABLETS. "**CUNEIFORM**" MEANS "**WEDGE-SHAPED**" BECAUSE THE REEDS CREATED WEDGE SHAPES IN THE CLAY.

THE SUMERIANS (EARLY MESOPOTAMIANS) INVENTED CUNEIFORM AROUND 3000 B.C.E. AT FIRST, IT WAS ALL VERY SIMPLE. WORDS FOR OBJECTS WERE JUST DRAWINGS OF THE OBJECTS THEMSELVES. FOR EXAMPLE, THE WORD FOR "FISH" WAS JUST A DRAWING OF A FISH. BUT CUNEIFORM EVOLVED UNTIL THE WRITING REPRESENTED SYLLABLES, NOT OBJECTS.

THIS IS—NO KIDDING!—AN **ACTUAL** RIDDLE FROM 1550 B.C.E., *TRANSLATED FROM CUNEIFORM:*

JOE, FRED, AND SAM
THE TIME WARP TRIO

"A HOUSE...
ONE ENTERS
IT BLIND,
ONE LEAVES
IT SEEING."

WHAT IS IT?

TURN THE PAGE UPSIDE DOWN TO REVEAL THE ANSWER.

ANSWER: A SCHOOL.

AND NOW BACK TO OUR STORY . . .

UMM, IT WAS IN MY ROOM.

AH, LET ME GUESS. YOU THREE ARE LOOKING FOR A BOOK, CORRECT?

HEY, WAIT! HOW DID YOU KNOW THAT?

I AM HAMMONRI, HIGH PRIEST OF THE GOD MARDUK. I SEE ALL THINGS.

IN THAT CASE, CAN YOU SEE HOW WE GET OUR BOOK BACK? FIRST A MONKEY HAD IT, THEN A MERCHANT, AND NOW THE QUEEN.

AMYITIS HAS IT, EH? I MEAN—

YES, I SEE HER CLEARLY! SHE IS IN THE—

HANGING GARDENS? THAT'S WHERE SHE SAID SHE WAS GOING.

YES! THE HANGING GARDENS, WHICH GREAT NEBUCHADNEZZAR BUILT FOR AMYITIS TO REMIND HER OF HER HOMELAND IN THE MOUNTAINS.

AND ON HER LAP IS A BLUE OBJECT WITH SILVER SQUIGGLES.

GO ON!

Eeeeeek!

THE BOYS CROSS A NARROW WOODEN PLANK . . .

Whoa!

. . . AND BARELY MAKE IT ACROSS!

SUDDENLY HAMMONRI GRABS THE WOODEN PLANK, REMOVING THE BOYS' ONLY EXIT.

Yoink!!

42

43

IN THE HANGING GARDENS . . .

SUCH A PRETTY A THING . . .

I WONDER WHERE IT'S FROM.

45

A PLACE CALLED BROOKLYN.

FORGIVE ME, MY QUEEN. I HAVE STARTLED YOU.

WHAT ARE YOU DOING IN THE GARDENS, HAMMONRI? SHOULDN'T YOU BE AT THE TEMPLE?

I CAME TO WARN YOU, MY QUEEN. THAT THING YOU HOLD IN YOUR HANDS IS *CURSED!* IF YOU OPEN IT, IT WILL BRING A *PLAGUE* UPON OUR LAND!

THIS THING?! OH, PLEASE! YOU'VE BEEN LISTENING TO TOO MUCH EPIC POETRY.

EVEN TOUCHING IT IS DANGEROUS! PERHAPS I SHOULD JUST HOLD IT FOR YOUR MAJESTY!

NO! NOW RUN ALONG. GO SACRIFICE SOMETHING.

AMYITIS TUCKS *THE BOOK* AWAY IN HER BAG.

LOOK!

A PINK IBIS!

HOW RARE!

AS AMYITIS TURNS AROUND, HAMMONRI SWITCHES HER BAG WITH HIS.

WHERE? I DON'T SEE ANYTHING.

Yoink!

NO? PERHAPS IT WAS A TRICK OF THE LIGHT. MAY MARDUK BLESS YOU WITH A HUNDRED SONS, AND NICE FAT COWS, AND—

BEFORE AMYITIS CAN SAY ANYTHING, HAMMONRI RUNS OFF.

48

FREDDI AND THE GUYS RUN OVER TO THE HANGING GARDENS TO FIND QUEEN AMYITIS.

MAN! CHECK OUT THE SIZE OF THIS THING!

NOW I SEE WHY THE HANGING GARDENS ARE ONE OF THE SEVEN WONDERS OF THE ANCIENT WORLD! IMAGINE THE ENGINEERING IT TAKES TO WATER ALL THOSE PLANTS!

COME ON, WE'RE WASTING TIME!

IMAGINE ALL THE STEPS WE'RE GONNA HAVE TO CLIMB. YOU THINK THEY BUILT AN ESCALATOR?

WE INTERRUPT THE STORY TO BRING YOU THIS MESSAGE . . .
THIS IS KING NEBUCHADNEZZAR II (TRY SAYING THAT FIVE TIMES FAST!) AND HIS WIFE, QUEEN AMYITIS.
KING NEBUCHADNEZZAR REBUILT THE CITY OF BABYLON AFTER IT WAS DESTROYED BY THE KING OF ASSYRIA. WHEN THE TIME WARP TRIO ARRIVED IN 580 B.C.E., IT WAS ONE OF THE BIGGEST AND MOST BEAUTIFUL CITIES IN THE WHOLE ANCIENT WORLD. HE BUILT THE TOWER OF BABEL . . .
. . . WHICH THE BABYLONIANS KNEW AS THE ZIGGURAT OF ETEMENANKI.
AND . . . DRUM ROLL, PLEASE . . .

The Famous

HANGING GARDENS
of Babylon!

AS THE STORY GOES, *QUEEN AMYITIS* MISSED THE AREA SHE GREW UP IN, WHICH WAS MOUNTAINOUS AND GREEN. SO THE KING BUILT A *VERTICAL* GARDEN, WITH MANY LEDGES AND OVERHANGS.

IRRIGATION TUNNEL

NO ONE KNOWS WHAT THE GARDENS ACTUALLY LOOKED LIKE, BUT BY ALL ACCOUNTS THEY WERE *HUGE*, LUSH, AND *REALLY HIGH TECH* FOR THEIR TIME. PUMPS, WHEELS, PULLEYS, AND TUNNELS WERE ALL USED TO KEEP EVERYTHING COLORFUL AND GREEN.

THE *HANGING GARDENS* WERE ONE OF THE SEVEN WONDERS OF THE ANCIENT WORLD.

AND NOW BACK TO OUR STORY . . .

54

WHAT IS IT NOW?!

OH, IT'S YOU. WHAT'S WRONG? IS MY HUSBAND BEING A TYRANT AGAIN?

NO, IT'S *THE BOOK*. WE REALLY NEED IT BACK!

THE WHAT?!

THAT THING YOU TOOK FROM US EARLIER. IF IT FALLS INTO THE WRONG HANDS, THE UNIVERSE COULD IMPLODE!

56

IF THE COBRA STRIKES, YOU WILL BE DEAD IN *MINUTES!*

HEY! I THINK I HAVE A PLAN.

YOU ARE *NOT* THROWING ME AGAIN!

WHOA!! THOSE CLARINET LESSONS REALLY PAID OFF!

FREDDI'S MAGNIFICENT FLUTE-PLAYING HYPNOTIZES THE COBRA.

THAT WAS AMAZING!

YOU ROCK!

YOU CHARMED THE SCALES OFF HIM!

YOU SAVED MY LIFE! HOW CAN I REPAY YOU?!

YOU CAN START BY TELLING US WHERE HAMMONRI WOULD BE.

THE POWER OF *THE BOOK* IS RELEASED.

FREDDI KNOWS THAT *THE BOOK* IN THE WRONG HANDS CAN CHANGE HISTORY FOREVER.

Hmmmmm . . . .

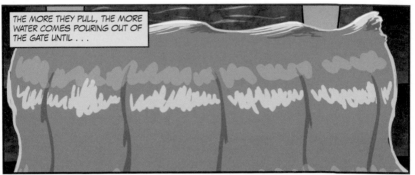

THE WATER FLOODS LEVEL AFTER LEVEL OF THE HANGING GARDENS UNTIL THE TOP TIER BEGINS TO SPRING A LEAK.

WH-WHAT'S GOING ON?

HAMMONRI TAKES HIS ATTENTION OFF *THE BOOK* FOR ONE SECOND, AND A STRONG GUST OF WIND BLOWS IT OUT OF HIS HANDS.

NO! COME BACK! COME BACK!

AT THE SAME TIME . . .

HURRY! THERE'S AN EXIT UP—

MUDSLIDE!

THERE GOES MY CHERRY ORCHARD.

UH, YOUR HIGHNESS? I THINK WE HAVE *BIGGER* PROBLEMS!

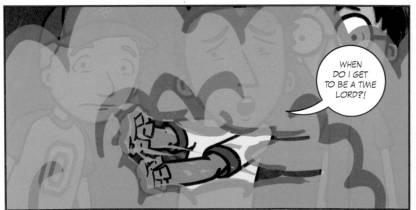

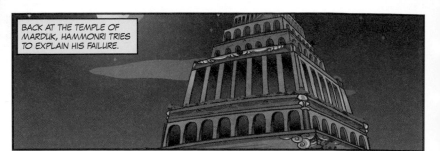

BACK IN THE PRESENT, FRED AND JOE TRY TO FIGURE OUT WHAT A *"TIME LORD"* IS, WHILE SAM TRANSLATES THE CLAY TABLET.

AHEM!

WELL?

IS IT JUST A SHOPPING LIST?

THIS FIRST LINE WAS REALLY HARD TO TRANSLATE.

SOME OF THE CHARACTERS ARE LIKE LITTLE PICTURES . . .

. . . WHILE OTHERS ARE LIKE LETTERS OF THE ALPHABET, SO I KEPT GETTING CONFUSED.

SAM! WHAT DOES IT SAY??

WELL, YOUR LORDSHIP, IT'S TIME FOR KING FRED TO BE HEADING HOME.

YOU COMING, SIR SAM?

WHY AM I JUST A "SIR"?

CAN'T I AT LEAST BE AN EARL OR . . .

THE END . . .

. . . OR IS IT?!